Or be a **pirate** my friends would fear.

I could be a ghost,
all floaty and light.

A skeleton with the
bones painted white.

Or a monstrous spider, a hair-raising sight!

My Bum is SO SPOOKY!

Dawn McMillan

ss Kinnaird

SCHOLASTIC

It's HALLOWEEN and I'm so **excited!**

It's my favourite time of the year.
I'd like to be **scary**, maybe wear something hairy.

But ...

Just wait and see
the *best* costume for me.

My friends are all here – a **clown** with a hat,
a **zombie**, a **werewolf**, and a **cute** purple bat.
The girl from next door looks like a **cat**.

My cousins are **vampires**
with capes and **big** teeth,

and make-believe **blood**
on their shirts underneath.

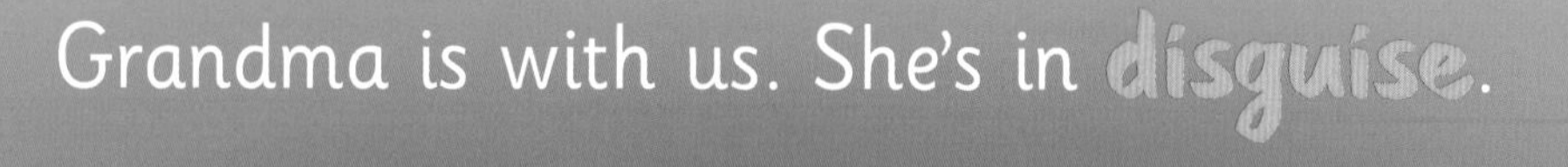
Grandma is with us. She's in disguise.

But ...

I have the **best**,
the most awesome
surprise!

Wait for the **squeals**,
the **shouts**,
and the **CRIES**
...

When everyone sees my …

BIG, SPOOKY BUM!

It's my **balloon!** I've tied it to me.
I've drawn a **scary** face, as you can see.

There's a row of **sharp** teeth, a nose that is **black!**
It looks like a **pumpkin** wearing a hat!

Now ... We walk down the street.
We have people to meet.

It's time to have **fun ...**
And we've just begun!

We have **frightful tricks**, ready to go.
Tricks that are **weird**. Tricks we can show.

Eyeball candies and smelly socks.

Party poppers with NOISY pops.

VAMPIRE smiles

and **DINOSAUR** teeth.

A **MUMMY** with
Cousin Tom underneath.

And that is not all ...

Guess who might
jump out
from behind a
brick wall?

We know **tricks** are fun
but we'd rather have treats
that fill up our pails
with lots of sweets.

Yes, our pails are filling
with **delicious** delights.
Lollipops, coloured **green**
and **white**.

Sweetie stars and
CHOCOLATE bars ...
So many goodies for Halloween
night.

And then ...

A Halloween party!

Fun, **spooky** treats and pale, ghostly eats!

Monster burgers with **eyeballs** on top.
Gummy worms that **wriggle** and **PLOP**.

Big, **scary** mouths with **big**, pointy teeth.
Long, witchy fingers
with sauce
underneath.

Games for us too.
Fun things to do …
MARSHMALLOW
monsters that swing on a string.

A **PIÑATA** and **ring toss**,

and ghost songs

to sing.

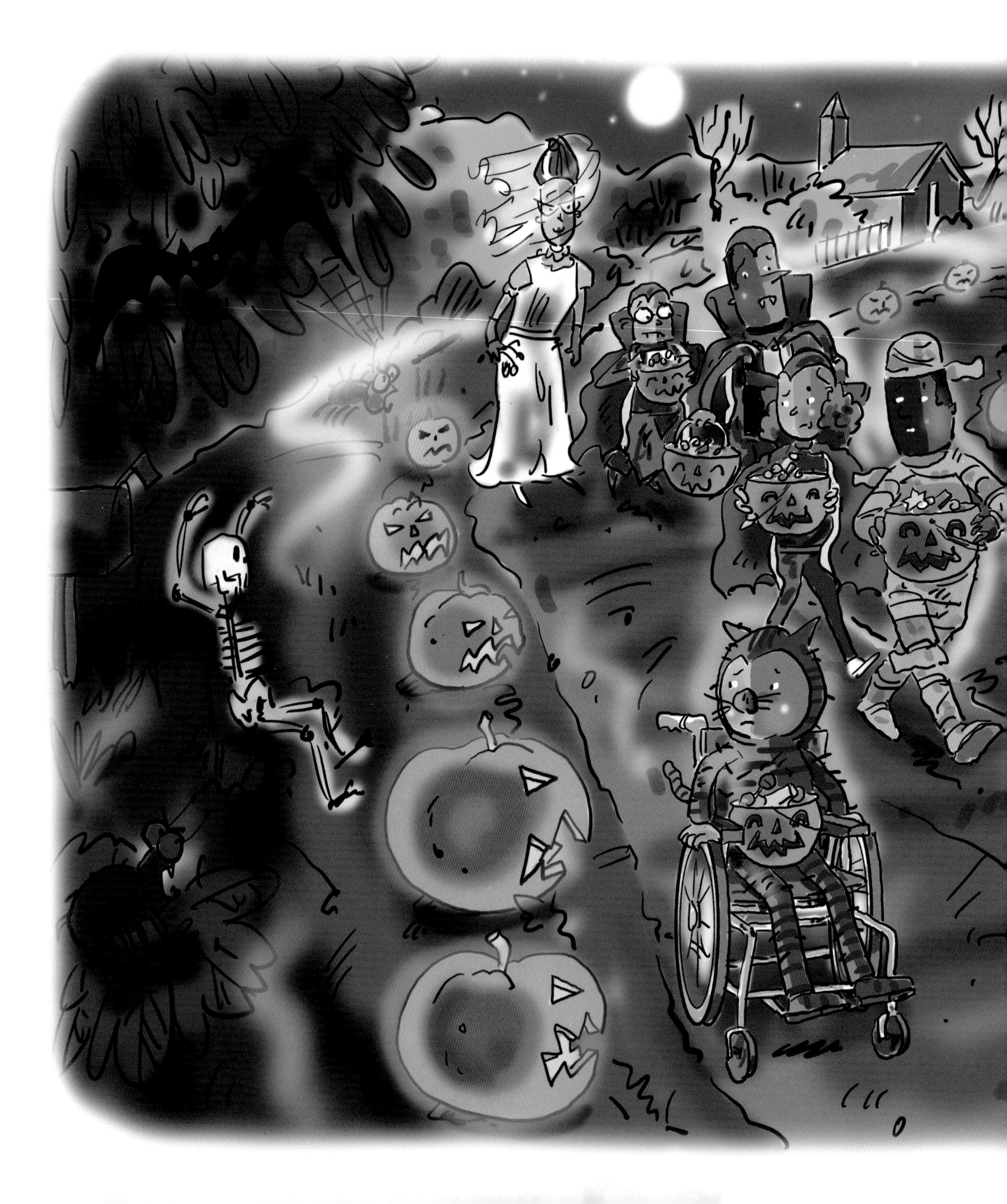

Oh no … time to go.

I've had lots of **fun**.

I'm taking my sweets home to share.

We walk very ***fast***.

We want to get past

the **pumpkin** faces that stare.

We walk through our door with sweets **galore**.
The pumpkins **glow** up on the shelf.

Our house is quite **creepy**.
Grandpa is sleepy.

And ...

Grandma is back to being herself.

Now I need to be **quick**
for *my* Halloween **trick**.

I'm busy **creating**.

The cousins are waiting …

I'm ready ...

I'm steady ...

Cousin Tom opens the door.
The **balloon** takes flight.

Up over our fence
and into the night!

It *floats* on the breeze
to *dance* past the trees!

There's **screaming** and squawking,

lots of **loud** talking!

Grandpa is **SHOUTING** the most.

And ...

Everyone is **gazing**

at something **amazing!**

It's my ...

BIG, SPOOKY
HALLOWEEN
GHOST!

About the author

Hi, I'm Dawn McMillan. I'm from Waiomu, a small coastal village on the western side of the Coromandel Peninsula in New Zealand. I live with my husband, Derek, and our cat, Lola. I write some sensible stories and lots of crazy stories! I love creating quirky characters and hope you enjoy reading about them.

About the illustrator

Hi, I'm Ross. I love to draw. When I'm not drawing, or being cross with my computer, I love most things involving the sea and nature. I also work from a little studio in my garden surrounded by birds and trees. I live in Auckland, New Zealand. I hope you like reading this book as much as I enjoyed illustrating it.

Published in the UK by Scholastic, 2023
1 London Bridge, London, SE1 9BG
Scholastic Ireland, 89E Lagan Road, Dublin Industrial Estate, Glasnevin, Dublin, D11 HP5F

First published in New Zealand by Oratia Media Ltd, 2023

ISBN 978 0702 32565 6

A CIP catalogue record for this book is available fr

Printed in Ita
Paper made from wood grown in sustainabl forests anc ... ces.

1 3 5 7 10 8 6 4 2

www.scholastic.co.uk